# Ruby's Dressed!

## Paul and Emma Rogers

little 🌳 ORCHARD

For Ruby — whatever she's wearing!

Other Ruby books for you to collect!
*Ruby's Potty*
*Ruby's Dinnertime*

ORCHARD BOOKS
96 Leonard Street, London EC2A 4XD
*Orchard Books Australia*
32/45-51 Huntley Street, Alexandria, NSW 2015
First published in Great Britain in 2003
First paperback publication in 2004
ISBN 1 84121 440 X (hardback)
ISBN 1 84362 290 4 (paperback)
Text © Paul Rogers 2003
Illustrations © Emma Rogers 2003
The right of Paul Rogers to be identified as the author and
Emma Rogers to be identified as the illustrator of this work
has been asserted by them in accordance with the
Copyright, Designs and Patents Act, 1988.
A CIP catalogue record for this book is available from the British Library.
(hardback) 1 2 3 4 5 6 7 8 9 10
(paperback) 1 2 3 4 5 6 7 8 9 10
Printed in Singapore

These are Ruby's favourite

matching pants and vest.

When Mummy puts these out for her,
She's happy to be dressed.

But if it's
any others,

Or if she wants to play,

Then just to get
her in her clothes
Can take up
half the day.

Now and then she chooses
To get dressed on her own.

"Ruby do it!"

she insists
And won't be helped or shown.

She's not
too good
with buttons,

And socks get in a knot.

With T-shirts
Ruby's never sure

Which hole is
meant for what.

Inside out or back to front,
She doesn't really care.

But both her feet inside one leg —
She's got a problem there!

She sometimes dresses Rabbit
To stop him feeling cold.

But even Rabbit
doesn't always
Do as he is told.

'Cos getting dressed is boring,

You do it and it's done.

It's not like dressing up – now that's

A **million** times more fun!

A patch and she's a pirate.

A crown and she's a queen.

A sheet and she's the scariest ghost

That you have ever seen!

She's wearing Daddy's slippers now,
Pretending she's a clown.

"Get your coat on," Mummy says, "We're going into town."

"Alright," says Mummy.
"But you still
need something
on your head."

Ruby's disappeared again.
What's she trying to find?

"Get a hat," says Mummy. "Come on, make up your mind."

But Ruby knows exactly

How she wants to dress.

"Are you ready?"
Mummy calls.
And Ruby answers . . .

"Yes!"